MW00876249

WRITERS REPUBLIC

YES, I love my hair!

Elijah Simmons

WRITERS REPUBLIC L.L.C.
515 Summit Ave. Unit R1
Union City, NJ 07087, USA

Website: *www.writersrepublic.com*
Hotline: *1-877-656-6838*
Email: *info@writersrepublic.com*

Ordering Information:
Quantity sales. Special discounts are available on quantity purchases by corporations, associations, and others. For details, contact the publisher at the address above.

Library of Congress Control Number: 2021917349
ISBN-13:   978-1-63728-707-1   [Paperback Edition]
                  978-1-63728-708-8   [Digital Edition]

Rev. date: 08/20/2021

This book is dedicated to every mother or grandmother
who ever had to maintain natural hair and to every young
girl who have yet to discover you are beautiful inside
and out. And last but not least to my Husband Maurice
for always encouraging me to love my natural hair.

Dedicated to every natural Girl and boy,
your hair is your natural crown

My name is Skye,

I am five years old and for all five of
those years' Mama says I have been
natural, which means keeping my hair
in its natural state and maintaining
it without any manmade chemicals.

Today is

M O N D A Y

and I am getting ready for school.
Monday is our busy day's which
means Mommy is in a rush and
I have to get my hair done.

My hair is

Brown, very fluffy and coily and

I love my hair.

"Skye"

Mama yells from the living room "It's time to do your hair, let's hurry we don't want to be late." My Mommy is a nurse at the local hospital.

As I sit down with Mommy,

she rubs her hands through my
hair. I can smell the oil on Mama's
hand's as she comb's my scalp and
gently reminds me why taking
care of my hair is so important.

After we're done, she
sends me off with

two big ponytails and a pretty pink bow

front and center afterwards we
head for the door before we get
there I stop and look in the mirror

"Well do you like it, Skye?"

Skye goes silent "Well Mama should we even try for a bow again, I hope it stays in this time" as she's rushing Grabbing her keys and heading for the door Mama smiles "of course we should my Skye."

Mama named her Skye because she is the air she breathes and the love she brings is like a breath of fresh air. "I love it Mama and I love my hair" Mama smiles and they head outside.

"There's the bus!"

I hug Mama and run toward the
end of the side walk. It starts to
rain as I head to the yellow bus.

"Bye Mama"

Skye shouts. Mama waves
her off and blows a kiss.
The rain has dampened
her fluffy hair.

The school bell rings and
Skye meets her friend
Izzy on the blacktop.

Izzy's real name is Isabella but she prefers Izzy, her hair is jet black and silky just like mine when it's straight during recess me and Isabella pretend to be princesses and let down our long hair. Only today mine was a little less silky.

My teacher blows her whistle
and we all run to the line
it's time to get ready to
pack up and go home.

The bus pulls up to our
front curb I see Mommy at
the door waiting for me.

"Hello my Skye, how was your day?".

Skye stopped in her tracks

"I want to be honest Mama,

it was kind of bad I think I had
a bad hair day, no matter where
I went or what I did everything
tried to destroy my hair."

29

Mama got down on my level, and said "your hair does not define you it's the beauty inside you that makes you special. "Well Mama you said to always maintain my crown "Skye replied very lost, Yes Skye but your crown is only as strong as the person wearing it. As long as you allow your inner beauty to shine your hair will always compliment it.

"I never thought about it that way, but I guess your right" Skye said as she twirled her puff balls in the same mirror she left so swiftly this morning, pulling at her frayed puffs. "Your right Mama I am beautiful inside and out and no matter rain or shine I love my hair.

Mama chuckled "That's right! Yes, you are Skye "Mama smiled and walked away to start dinner; Skye was embarrassed at how defeated she felt earlier that day. She decided from that day on that she would always love her natural hair whether brown, wet, fluffy, or, coily and tell them

"yes I love my hair".

CPSIA information can be obtained
at www.ICGtesting.com
Printed in the USA
BVRC101013050921
616108BV00004B/49

* 9 7 8 1 6 3 7 2 8 7 0 7 1 *